BERNIE
The One-Eyed Puppy

written by
SALLY KURJAN

Illustrated by
SHANNARA HARVEY

Bernie wasn't like his brothers and sisters. They were all born with two eyes, a nose, a hungry little mouth, four legs, and a waggy tail.

When all the
other puppies
opened their
eyes, they saw
that Bernie only
had one eye.

And, Bernie's front legs were not like theirs. His were curvy and bendy instead of nice and straight.

Even though no one else could tell,
Bernie's heartbeat was not like his
brothers and sisters, either. He got
tired very quickly when they played
and had to rest often.

Bernie's mama loved him very much and told him he would find a wonderful family to take care of him. He loved his mama and knew she was right.

When all the other puppies were taken to the pet store to find a home, Bernie didn't go with them.

Instead, he was given to a nice lady who had a houseful of puppies! They ran all around the living room and had lots of toys!

Bernie really liked the nice lady. She laughed a lot and was fun to play with. She told him she would find a good home for him.

Every day people came to the house to see the puppies. Bernie would run up to them and smile when they said how cute he was.

Then, they would notice that he only had one eye, and they would say, "Ewww," or "Yuck."

Bernie didn't know what those words meant, but it made him sad when the people didn't want him.

The nice lady kept telling him that he was a special puppy and that he would find a happy home.

Days and days and days went by. The other puppies in the foster home were leaving one by one. But nobody wanted little one-eyed Bernie.

Then one day it happened!
When someone knocked on the door,
Bernie ran as fast as he could and
jumped on the lady who had come to
see him.

She scooped him
up and hugged
and kissed him.
She didn't say any
mean words at
all! The man and
boy with her were
nice and they said
kind things too!

Next thing Bernie knew, he was leaving the nice lady's home. He rode in the backseat of the car with the boy. The boy kept saying nice words to him.

Finally they stopped at a pretty house. The lady said, "Bernie, you are home!" The boy let him run in the green grass and it tickled his tummy.

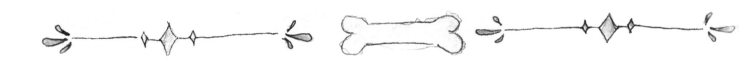

Bernie was in for another surprise! His new brother came outside to meet him. Spike gave him a funny look, but he licked his ear and said, "Let's play!"

Spike was a little different too, so Bernie's one-eyed face didn't bother him at all. He thought Bernie was fun and cute. It worried him, though, when Bernie had to rest after playing for a few minutes.

After getting to know Spike, the lady said, "Now you can meet the rest of your family," and introduced him to Bella and Ubu.

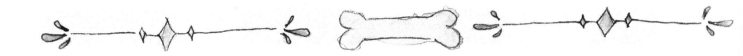

Bella was the most beautiful dog Bernie had ever seen, other than his mama. He thought she must surely be a princess!

Ubu was not pretty like Bella, and he was not friendly like Spike. He growled when Bernie came too close, and Bernie was frightened of him.

The lady told Ubu to be nice, but he didn't want to be friends with Bernie. He had never seen a puppy that looked like Bernie.

Bernie wanted Ubu to like him. He ran around the living room to show Ubu how fast he was. He made funny puppy faces. He gave Ubu one of his new puppy toys.

Ubu still did not seem to like Bernie. By this time, Bernie was so sleepy that he just wanted a cozy place to take a nap.

He snuggled up next to Ubu and fell sound asleep. Ubu looked at the little one-eyed, crooked legged puppy and decided he wasn't so bad after all. In fact, he was very sweet.

When Bernie woke up, the lady
kissed his face and told him she
loved him just how he was. His little
smile said that he loved her too!

Bernie was happier than he had
ever been in his whole life.
He loved his new family and they all
loved him too. Even Ubu!

CPSIA information can be obtained
at www.ICGtesting.com
Printed in the USA
JSHW020741290120
3875JS00001B/2

9 780692 138526